THE LATE WORK OF

MARGARET KROFTIS

THE LATE WORK OF
MARGARET KROFTIS

A NOVELLA BY
MARK GLUTH

LITTLE HOUSE
ON THE BOWERY

AKASHIC BOOKS
NEW YORK

Also from Dennis Cooper's
Little House on the Bowery Series

The Show That Smells
by Derek McCormack

High Life
by Matthew Stokoe

Userlands: New Fiction Writers from the Blogging Underground
edited by Dennis Cooper

Artificial Light
by James Greer

Wide Eyed
by Trinie Dalton

Godlike
by Richard Hell

The Fall of Heartless Horse
by Martha Kinney

Grab Bag
by Derek McCormack

Headless
by Benjamin Weissman

Victims
by Travis Jeppesen

This is a work of fiction. All names, characters, places, and incidents are the product of the author's imagination. Any resemblance to real events or persons, living or dead, is entirely coincidental.

The chapter titled "The Emptiest Place in the Circle" is named after a line from the song "Love Is Stronger Than Witchcraft" by Robert Pollard, from the album *From a Compound Eye;* the epigram that opens the first chapter of this book is one of the five remembrances of Buddhism, it's from no specific text; the epigram that opens the second chapter is from the song "Stadiums and Shrines II" by Sunset Rubdown, from the album *Shut Up I Am Dreaming*; the epigram that opens the third chapter is from the story "The Theologians" by Jorge Luis Borges.

Published by Akashic Books

ISBN-13: 978-1-933354-94-1
Library of Congress Control Number: 2009922940

First printing

Little House on the Bowery
c/o Akashic Books
PO Box 1456
New York, NY 10009
info@akashicbooks.com
www.akashicbooks.com

Sincerest thanks to: Barbara and Edward Gluth, Erin Kelly, David Hatch, Dennis Cooper, Johnny Temple, Joel Westendorf, Michelle Zuber, Nicholas Rhodes, Nicky Smith, the Detroit Film Center, and *Ellipsis* magazine (Wayward Couch Press).

For Buster and Clarence

CHAPTER 1
THE LATE WORK

All that is dear to me and everyone I love are of the nature to change. There is no way to escape being separated from them.

—Buddha

PART I
RAINER

MARGARET'S SITTING AT HER writing table, then walking downstairs to put a kettle on. A dog walks in the kitchen behind her and yawns. Outside the window the weather's a film of the seasons changing. Those are geese flying south. Upstairs, she's no longer cold. It's the tea. The dog turns three tight circles and lies down on the rug he's mushed up against the wall. Margaret's working on a piece of fiction. It's autobiographical in a sense. She dies in the end.

She goes into town to buy groceries. The sidewalks are covered with fallen leaves. They're trying to become a forest floor, she thinks. At the store she buys cans of soup and bread instead of ingredients. On the way back to her car she sees the bay. It looks like it goes on forever. For a moment she imagines the world like that: just the ocean and the weather.

After dinner she writes three sentences. They're not worth keeping, she thinks. She lets the dog out one last time then dries him off because he's soaked.

She brushes her teeth and gets in bed. He burrows under the sheets and rests his black head on her feet. In her dream he can see ghosts.

The sun rises. It burns away the mist and the fog. Margaret watches the steam spin through the branches. The world's closed, the sky's a roof. Those are her thoughts. She sweeps up the oil seeds and millet from the porch. She sprays her hose at the eaves and the windows. Her hands are freezing from the water. She calls the dog. He runs up. She wraps her arms around his barrel chest and rests her head on his twitching back. She whispers in his ear as she tries to get him to hold still.

Margaret sticks her hand under the faucet in the kitchen. She slices an apple, drinks from a water glass. The dog eats a cracker, she takes something out of the microwave. Margaret eats and cleans up. She lies down on the couch, a shadow across the ceiling. A bird makes a sound outside. She thinks it's kids playing. There are no kids near here. She remembers something that she's holding onto. She tells herself that she will never forget it.

Margaret goes for a walk down by the water. A plastic bag washes up on the shore and gets caught on a wormy log. She picks it up. It's tangled with seaweed.

She leans on her cane and thinks. The rain's suspended between the sky and everything else. The fog smudges the horizon.

Later, back up the path, she smells something. Twenty feet farther she can see in her kitchen window and it's so horrible.

Margaret's in the hotel room insurance put her in. She cries so hard she coughs, lies down on the bed, and makes a fist. She wants to punch herself like a wall.

They let her walk through what's left of her house. The fire gutted most of the ground floor. Upstairs, her office was largely untouched, her notebooks and computer.

Back downstairs, in the kitchen, her fingers are trembling. She's kneeling in front of the backdoor. She's memorizing the gouges his claws made in it as he tried to escape.

PART 2

3 DREAMS

I

WE WERE WALKING ON A TRAIL *that I didn't recognize. You humored me and didn't pull on your lead. We walked through a field then entered a forest. The trees blocked the sun. The trail followed down into a valley. Fog rolled in and I thought of an owl. My foot slipped on loose gravel and we fell into a cave. It'd been hidden by brush. I landed on my ankle and you landed on your head. You yelped and shrieked and I dragged myself across the cold and wet floor. A pool of blood ranged wide around your head. I loosened your collar. I petted your face and smoothed your ears back. I looked into your eyes. They told me that you were scared, strong, sad, wistful, doubtful, confused, brave, and in pain. I told you I loved you. I told you how sorry I was. The words were worthless because whatever hope they came from was unfounded. You tried to bark and instead gasped for breath. Your leg began shaking like you were fighting something, then your whole body. I was overcome. I laid over you so you would feel protected and less scared. I hoped you couldn't tell I was weeping. You became a memory.*

2

You were floating in the ocean. You were dying, then dead. Something had happened to you. I didn't know. It was just your body. It was bloated and distended. I was swimming alongside of it. I was still trying to save you. There wasn't a chance in the world. Then I was standing on the shore. I could barely walk in my clothes. Your fur was slack over your shrunken bones, your bottom jaw was missing. Crabs crawled through your sand-matted fur. Your body was lying in a shallow pool. I kicked seaweed over you. I couldn't think. It was what made sense in that moment. The tide washed it away. Your body moved with the water as it flowed in and out. You were stirring then still. I fell to my knees. I scooped up filthy sand with my hands. I poured it all over you. I thought that I could hide your body from the circling birds. I gave up. They would scavenge your corpse no matter what I did.

3

It was night and I was walking you through the neighborhood where David and I used to live. It was our first house together. This was twenty years before you were born. We were walking slowly. The cars in the driveways were covered with ice. I walked through a puddle and it splashed on my pants. My feet were soaked. You sniffed at something. You just stood there. It warmed up. The wind began to blow. My hood fell back. My hair fell in my face and got into my eyes. You were panting. It seemed like you were smiling. I looked at your face. I looked into your eyes. There was so much there. The moment was frozen. Everything lasted forever. Then you took off. The lead ran through my fingers. There was no way that I could react. There were trees and wetlands and empty fields behind the houses. That's what you disappeared into. It was like a thousand miles away. I just knew it was impossible to find you. I knew that I would never see you again.

Part 3
Months Later

Margaret bites the fingernail on her left pinky. She takes a sip of cold tea then sets the cup on the saucer and picks up her notebook. She's working on her short story. She tells herself it'll be the last thing she writes. She's working on a short passage about her dog. Including him in the story is the most important thing in the world. In her latest draft she put him on a boat, surrounded by water. There's no way a fire could suffocate him there. But she realizes it's ridiculous. So the boat sinks and the inconceivable happens anyway. She still sobs as she falls asleep at night.

She sets down her pencil and leans back. She rests her eyes for a moment, then dabs at them with her handkerchief. Her hand's numb. It's shaking. She rubs her wrist but that doesn't do anything. She's going to take a nap, she thinks. After that, she'll work on the story a little more.

The officer knocked, got no response, then found the

spare key the neighbor talked about. It was on an old necklace, hanging from the rhododendron next to the porch. He walked upstairs and into the bedroom. He called out to the shape under the covers. When he touched her face it was like ice. He closed her eyes and called for an ambulance. While he was waiting he walked into the next room. Beside the computer he found a small stack of papers. He read them.

My Watery Death

by Margaret Kroftis

I was down by the water. Someone said my name, and when I turned around to answer, I saw a boy standing in front of me. He introduced himself and apologized. He said he'd knocked for five minutes before coming around the back. I told him not to worry. He told me that he'd come to ask me to read his story and give him advice about writing. The sky behind him was white but it looked black reflected on the water. He bit his lip. I told him I could have the story read in a couple days then watched the rain pool on his hood. He handed me the manila envelope he'd been holding and the pool fell past his face and dissolved into the sand. I watched him as he trotted up toward my house and then disappeared behind the garage.

Inside, my footsteps left puddles the shape of continents on old maps. They evaporated while I ate dinner. I read magazines in the bath, then, in bed, the boy's story. It was ten loosely organized pages describing an army of demons attacking the earth via a porthole to another dimension. The next morning I wrote down my dream. In it, I was standing in the kitchen looking out the window onto the water. It was dark but I could see that the water was luminescent, like it was lit from within.

A week later the boy arrived in the rain on his bike. Inside, the steam from the kettle scalded my fingers as I made tea. At the table I held some ice cubes wrapped in a tea towel and told the boy that I didn't know anything about horror, that I didn't know if I'd be able to help him with his writing.

He said, "But isn't all writing the same, I mean, in the end?"

The boy told me where to drive. We turned left out of my driveway and headed north.

He had me pull over next to a trailhead that was overgrown by snowberries. We followed it until we came upon a clearing where the boy climbed a boulder. It was rounded and smooth because eventually it will be nothing. From behind the trees ahead of me I heard the drone of cars driving on the freeway. It reminded me of an overcast sky which reminded me of my childhood.

The boy brought me to the clearing to help explain his writing. He told me he fell asleep here once, lying on the boulder, and when he woke up he had the entire plot for his story in his head. His thought was that I would understand the tone he was going for if I came here. He opened the thermos and poured himself some tea. I had a daydream in which my ears were so sensitive that they could hear the tea evaporating. He sat on the boulder and cupped his mug in both hands. I walked around the clearing then scratched at some stinging nettle on my calf.

Then November. Each day mirrored the previous one: breakfast and coffee, then yard work until my energy disappeared. Nap, then dinner, then soaking in the tub. Bed. Once a week the boy came and we talked about his writing and the work he was doing.

One night I dreamed that a ship sank in the middle of the ocean and all the passengers drowned except for a dog. The dog swam until his muscles became numb, and then began to ache. As the sun set he stopped chasing the birds that he would never catch and tried to move toward the reflection of the moon on the water. His muscles gave up and he stopped swimming. Water coursed down his throat and he was blinded as time and his suffering stopped.

The boy told me he thought he'd never finish his story. I told him I thought that with everything I had ever written, that it was normal. He smiled, and asked me why I didn't write anymore. I told him I didn't have the time. I realized the boy had read my novel but knew nothing about me. He didn't seem to know about my retirement, mastocytosis, anything. As he was about to leave, he asked me if there was something he could do to repay me for my help. I asked him if he had a boat.

I was sitting at the kitchen table reading the

boy's story. Several months' worth of work had improved it. The demons had been replaced by a vague and malevolent cosmic force that was causing a gradual apocalypse on earth. It was now written as a series of diary entries by a teenage girl, one of the last survivors left. In the section I was reading, the narrator was huddled in her bedroom. It had been pitch dark for the past three days and she'd not seen anyone else in two weeks. She was scared to leave her house. She used a flashlight to look out the window. The trees around her house were growing taller and thicker. The clearing was shrinking. She couldn't see the moon. She was worried it was gone. She knew that clearing would soon vanish. She feared for what would happen when the unstoppable occurred. She paced around the house. She hid under the bed. She finished the last of the cereal that she had. She still felt hungry. She began turning the dial on her clock radio. She looked for some signal She found an automated emergency response broadcast, it said that the earth had stopped spinning on its axis. The girl lay down and started crying. She missed her parents but had no hope of ever seeing them again.

The boy paced between the stove and sink as I finished his story. In it, the narrator fell asleep as the world slowly disappeared. She had a dream she was dead and that her ghost was traveling around the earth. I underlined the last sentence: *The trees are like wisps, and I can float through them, but they seem even less there than they were yesterday.* I told him he should be proud of it and he smiled.

After lunch the boy and I walked down to the water and got in his kayak. He rowed us through mist that became drizzle. It beaded on my skirt and clouded my glasses. There was barely any breeze and the air smelled like the sea, and diesel. The boy rowed and I daydreamed that the water was a black hole. I slipped through space and into it.

CHAPTER 2
JOYFUL THING

I'm sorry anybody dies.
—Spencer Krug

Part I
Jyfl Thng

BETH LOOKS OUT THE WINDOW AND squints. The sky hangs from the trees. It's just ink in water. She looks for a message in it. If it's there it's too complex. It all just washes over her. She looks at the notebook lying open on her lap. She's working on the script she's writing. It's based on a story by Margaret Kroftis. In it, Margaret helps a teenage boy write a story about the end of the world. Then she commits suicide. It touches Beth. She can't say why. She feels like she's falling. She takes a breath. She writes a sentence, crosses it out. Her mind's just something else in the world. Like a wolf, like an ocean. It twitches and unlocks. She thinks about the film she plans to make, how it will come together. She thinks about how it will embody what an amazing writer Margaret was. She thinks it will be like a memorial or whatever.

She hears the door to the garage open. Her mom calls her name. She walks downstairs, hugs her.

I bought groceries, do you want to eat?

They're sitting at the table.

Salad, cool.

She reaches for a piece of bread. Her mom asks her what she's doing.

Um, writing.

She asks what it's about. Her voice is crunchy and muffled.

Uh, I dunno, it's kinda complicated.

Wrapped In Plastic are practicing in Peter's garage. J paces in front of the garage door. Peter zones out on his synthesizer. J sings. Declan breaks a drumstick. He stops playing his hi-hat. That fucks Peter up. He falls out of time with the sequencer. J tosses his notebook down. He heads out the side door. Peter hears the phone ringing. He runs inside to get it. It's Beth. She sounds like she just swallowed something. Peter guesses grapefruit juice. She asks him if he wants to get something to eat. There's something in her voice. She says she'll pick him up. She asks him if he could drive. Her eyes are acting weird again. He lets her go. He thinks whatever about the band. He walks back into the garage. Declan's wrapping his hand in an Ace bandage. He's duct taping the toe of his sneaker. Peter finds J outside smoking Drum. J throws a rock at some birds on the fence. He misses by three feet. Peter says he'll have to get going soon. He says J and Declan could stay and play if they want. J says that Declan only has one drumstick. He says that it's not worth it. He doesn't say everything. Peter doesn't say anything.

The lights reflect in Beth's glasses. They dive and blur. Peter sees something there, then nothing. A strand of Beth's hair falls forward. She smooths it back. She says something. He giggles, she smiles. He looks into her eyes. They finish the pot of tea. They make out in the car. It's colder than they realized. They wipe off the windows. As he drives he puts his arm around her. She kisses his fingers and presses her face against them. He yawns. She rests her head on his shoulder. He pulls in front of his house and kills the engine. The rain on the windshield gives the streetlights halos. A car drives slowly past them. He plays with her ponytail. The moon's low in the sky. The cloud next to it lends it gravity. Beth closes her eyes. Only she and Peter exist.

J walks up to Peter's locker. He hands him a couple pages ripped out of a notebook.

Don't lose these.

Peter looks through them in History class. They're J's plans for Wrapped In Plastic's live show. In the line drawing he's studying, Declan's drum kit is set up perpendicular to the audience. They're just a wash of pencil lead. The lines aimed at them are spotlights.

Peter turns the page. He reads a list of song titles, then lyrics. He grabs a pen out of his pocket. He draws a cube. It's three-dimensional, a dumb trick he learned. After school he hangs out in J's bedroom. He coughs, asks J to roll him a cigarette. Peter says he likes the lyrics. J says thanks, he says they're horrible. J sips his cup of coffee. Peter closes his eyes and buzzes. He's so dizzy. He holds the cigarette up to the window. J's in the corner. His desk is a piece of plywood on saw-horses. He's drawing a pentagram on a scan of a Beatrix Potter drawing. He's trying to make a poster. The sharpie's running out of ink. The scribble looks like a rainy sky.

Beth calls Peter. She asks him about school. He says it was fine. He tells her that he wishes he wasn't there. Her English teacher gave them a huge assignment. She'll have to work on it over break, she says. She asks him if he wants to come over.

He peers into her fridge. She rinses out a cereal bowl in the sink.

My mom will be home soon. I promised her I'd help her with her homework.

Peter empties a glass of juice into his mouth. Beth puts her arm around his waist.

But you could just hang out in my room.

They wake up late for school. She pulls on pants

and splashes water on her face. He rubs toothpaste on his teeth with his finger. They run downstairs, get in his car, figure *fuck it*, and drive downtown. They eat breakfast at a Starbucks. He draws a picture of them on a napkin. They hold hands as they walk down the street. He spends money he doesn't have on a dress for her. They steal postcards from a bookstore because a clerk was giving them dirty looks. They walk to a park. They sit on a bench by the water. The sky's pink and gray. Everything's clear. His hands are freezing. Her eyes tear in the wind. She closes them. She buries her face in his sweater. Her head rests on his shoulder. The world spins and she opens her eyes. Islands or mountains hang on the horizon. She takes off her scarf and wraps it around Peter's head. She wishes she had a camera. He's such a cute mummy.

J's upstairs in his room smoking cigarettes and playing guitar. Outside it's night and damp. A breeze comes through the screen. The room looks yellow because of the lampshade. He walks away from it and slumps on his bed. The window helps him breathe. He stares at the TV on his desk. It blurs, then un. The static is just sound. He gulps from his cup. Coffee grounds coat his tongue and throat. He gags and presses play. The tape of what he was playing plays. It's three minor key chords. They're all flanged and hissed. They repeat forever. Whatever it is, it fails at everything he was aiming for. He punches the button until the tape ejects. He hucks it across the room. It gets so quiet his ears start ringing. He chews his thumbnail. It begins to bleed. He rolls a cigarette. It tastes off, something in his throat. He grabs his notebook and a pencil. He tries to write some lyrics. He looks at the open notebook. There's nothing there. He feels something drop inside. His numb shoulders crumble beneath the weight. He buries his face in the carpet. He swings his head back and forth. What that makes his eyes see is so much more interesting than anything else. Everything he knows becomes something different. It disappears.

Beth wakes up and scoots up on the couch. She kisses Peter's cheek then walks out to her car. On her way home she thinks about the goofy face he was making as he slept. In bed she dreams that she's kissing him. When she wakes up she's tangled in her blanket. At school she runs up to him and hugs him from behind. During first period he draws a picture of her in his notebook. She finds it slipped into her locker at lunch. When she gets home she tapes it to her mirror. Its flaws are hidden behind the charm of his non-technique. She tries to write a poem for him in return but words fail her. It comes to nothing.

* * *

J paces. He winces at the sun then walks inside. To him school is nothing because there's nothing there for him to wrap his head around. Hence that look in his eyes. He walks upstairs. Clocks click. The doors are windows. He's watching a tree do this trick. It moves so slowly in the wind. The teacher talks, talks. He's tapping the tip of his pencil against the back of his fingers, against the nails. He counts. The kid next to him kicks his chair. He looks up, loses concentration. The barrel slips through the tips of his fingers. Blood from his thumb covers the bottom of his desk. He pulls the pencil out. Something resists, breaks off. He grabs his wrist and stands up. He looks at the dizzy lights, the teacher. She just doesn't have time to deal with his bullshit such as she sees it. Someone snickers. Ahead of him in the hall are just these walls and lockers and paint and the smell of soap. The secretary takes one look at his hand and sends him to the nurse. She puts on gloves. She washes off the sticky blood. He closes his eyes and she pulls the lead out. She drops it on a cotton ball, puts that in the sink. He holds his hand above his heart. She wraps up his thumb. She gives him an ice pack. She lets him nap on the couch. When he wakes up he can't feel his hand. He's so freaked out. She tells him it's okay. She tells him it will get better. He tells her that he didn't know what happened. That makes him start to cry. She takes a step forward. She comes around her desk. It's just what she was doing. Maybe it's her smile. He sees something behind it, so much that he can't decode. She's talking to him. He just takes off. The trophy case is the dumb background as he runs for the side door. The hall's empty, the parking lot. When he slows down he can think. He puts his hands on his knees. He looks up. Cars are stuck in traffic, the clouds are puffy like pictures. He coughs from the running. There's so much he doesn't know. He's just a wreck like everyone else.

Declan e-mails Peter and J. He wants to know if they can practice Monday or Tuesday. *Let me know*. Peter replies, *Tuesday*. There's nothing from J. Beth comes over with popcorn and red licorice. They sit on the couch and watch TV. His dad tells them J called. She finds *The Shining* playing somewhere. The commercials ruin it. She falls asleep. He wakes her up when her mom calls. She waves to him when he drops her off. He calls her when he gets home. He'd promised. He tells her he made it home safe. She's asleep. She doesn't remember. He drinks one of his dad's beers to get tired. When he closes his eyes he sees lights flashing in time with his heartbeat. They're just there. He squeezes his eyes tight. They erupt. White light takes over everything. It's all there is.

* * *

J leads Peter and Beth through the parking lot. The hurricane fencing's rusted and rattling. The wind's cold. It throws the darkness. Beth hugs her jacket around herself. She shrugs into the collar. Peter watches J climb the pile of crates and boxes. They shake as he balances. Peter kills the flashlight. He thought he saw something. J snaps at him. He says that he might as well be fucking blind. His face is streaked with soot. It's from the windows. The soles of his boots slap the ground as he jumps down. He takes off around the other side of the building. Some lights on poles shine. It's okay. He picks a crowbar off the ground. The door wrenches as he pries at the latch. They all run inside. They're out of breath when they stop. They sit down on a conveyor belt. Peter coughs. J rolls a cigarette. Beth lies back. Her hair falls away from her face and through the rollers. Something flies across the building. It disappears out a broken window. It freaks Beth out. She tells herself it was so far away. She tells herself it didn't matter. She pulls a bottle of gin out of her pocket. Some spills on her skirt as she slurps from it. She laughs and swigs. She's this buzzy thing. She closes her eyes and rolls her head onto Peter's shoulder. The world collapses around her. She has this daydream: curtains for everything. It was something about the building and the booze. They came together. She begins to cry. She sobs silently. J's talking to Peter. They don't notice. J says the roof's so high. He says that the building has its own weather. He swears. Peter shines the light straight up. He pulls on the bottle Beth handed him. A thin cloud mists the ceiling. Maybe it's just the shadows and the light. An old blimp hangs against the wall. It's only one part that they see. It's so enormous. Water pools beneath it. That's one of the sounds. Peter hoots. He taps a clicky beat on the floor with his feet. The wind picks up and they're sprayed by something. The cold moves quickly through all the missing windows. It startles Beth. Her eyes blur and spin. Everything disappears except for Peter's voice. He's talking to J. They're talking about a video. Peter says that Declan has a camera, that all they would need are lights. J says that it's so safe here, that no one will find them. He says that it's like it doesn't exist.

A storm comes in. The clouds shift and run. The wind throws rain through the screen of an open window. Beth closes it. She's too fascinated to write. She stares at the hummingbird beneath the eaves. She lies down on a blanket on the kitchen floor. She looks out the sliding door. The trees sway. They turn darker. Sheets of rain run down the window. The world fades. The clock on the microwave flicks off. She tries the light switch. She puts her head down. She closes her eyes.

The air sits thick as she sleeps. She wakes up suddenly. It was her back. She was turned funny. The furnace is on. She walks stiffly to the couch. She rests her face in her hands. She grabs her notebook, her mother's laptop. She types her script up, or tries to. She thinks that this is the final draft. She's rewritten each sentence until it's invisible. She wishes she was a better writer. She wishes it came more easily. She's thinking of the film she wants to make. She has no idea how to do it. Thus her lack of self-confidence. Thus her panic. She reads a couple lines out loud. Her mind moves faster than her lips. Her pen snaps. She didn't realize she'd been bending it.

The phone rings. It's Peter. She talks to him. He tells her she's so smart. He tells her that if she writes a script she'll be able to make a movie. He tells her it won't be a problem.

Why don't you finish it later? I could come over.

She walks out to meet him in the driveway. It's dark. The breeze is colder than she thought. The wind blows the rain off a tree. A cat paws at a puddle by the curb. It takes off then stops. A car's coming up. It circles in the headlights. It's a possum. Beth and Peter walk around the side of the house. They're on the patio. He sits on the bench that circles the tree. She goes inside. The moon and the sound of a car somewhere. Peter tries to count the stars. He loses his place. He decides it has to be infinite. Beth comes back with two glasses of wine. She sits on his lap, tips a glass to his lips. He almost chokes, coughs. They laugh. She leans backwards against his arm. He misses her mouth. Her hoodie is drenched and purple. She takes it off and wrings it out on the patio. He grabs her hand and kisses her. He puts his arm around her waist. They stumble inside, then upstairs.

Peter can't sleep. He leans up in bed. He grabs the glass of wine from Beth's nightstand. She turns over. She just slays him. He leans up against the pillow and downs the glass. His hair gets in his eyes. He squints, she dissolves. The clock's the only light. He touches her shoulder. He closes his eyes. He has a dream that they're walking together. They're standing in a field. It's raining. Their clothes, hair, and faces are soaked. He starts to cry. He's overcome. He can't explain. He tells her he loves her so much. Beth holds him. He pulls the covers over them and then disappears into sleep. The moment moves on.

J has this dream. He's in the warehouse. He steps through puddles. The ground's covered in ice. The roof's wrecked. It's raining inside. It's full of trees and light. It's all frozen and slippery. He has all these thoughts. They're ponderous and failed. Waves wash over him, through him. A bird flies overhead. Its call makes it seem bigger than it is. J gets scared. He disappears behind a sheet of Visqueen. It was caught in some branches. It was just hanging there. He presses his face against it. He blinks, steps back, forward. He can't make anything out. The blurry dark's wide as his eyes. It looks like complexity to his auteuresque mind.

Beth's riding her bike. Peter's walking with her. It's so cold she's barely moving. Her peddling's really just these slow strides. She tells him that she's sick of it being dark all the time. She says she hates the winter. He just looks at her. He stops moving. She can feel the cold in her ears and throat. She tells him he looks handsome. He can't see her mouth. It's the scarf. Her eyes smile. They get to her house. They kiss in the driveway. Beth tells him he feels warm. She pulls herself up against him. She tells him to come over later. They walk up on the porch. She leaves her bike outside. She begins humming a song. She doesn't realize it. Peter turns around. From the front window Beth can see almost the whole street. She watches him as he walks, his hands in his pockets, disappearing after the streetlight.

J's in bed then at his desk. He fills a dozen pages with pen drawings. Each line is whatever, the spaces are what makes them compelling. At least to his mind. He pauses. He reads his e-mail, shuts off his computer. He's convinced that there was something to his dream. That's what the drawings are of. He thinks they will form a whole thing. Like a novel or an album. He picks up the phone and tries to call Peter. It rings too many times. He hangs up. He looks out the window. The clouds are mountains, amoebas. The light on the horizon is god to someone. J looks down at his notebook. He leans back. His thoughts are a reeling crawl. He closes his eyes and pretends there's something there. It connects everything to everything else.

Peter's asleep. Beth's kissing his ear. She fidgets, grabs her notebook.

I see you, do you see me? Of course not.

She draws him a picture. The sky's above them in it. It looks so stupid, she thinks. She shakes him until he wakes up. They walk outside so she can show him the moon. He takes his camera out of his pocket. He tries to take a picture. It's all black, it sucks. It gets colder. It begins to snow. The lens is too weak, or the moon. He gives up. They turn and walk inside. The snowflakes stay in her hair and shine in the light on the porch. They're just water in her eyes once they walk inside.

J's in the library making copies. His drawings don't

come through. They lose whatever it was that made them. He leaves them there. After school he shows one to Peter. It was a tree before he obliterated it. He looks for something in Peter's eyes. He smiles. Peter says *cool,* then takes off for Beth's car. When J gets home he hangs out in the garage. His mom pulls in the driveway, she doesn't notice him. All his focusing has wrecked his mind. He's stressed out. He smokes three cigarettes. He watches the snow. The backyard's usually nothing to think of but the snow does something. It merges everything together. It makes him feel like a child. J sits down on the milk crate at his feet. The ridges push through his jeans. They kill his ass. It doesn't matter. He tries not to cough. He sneezes and rubs at his burning eyes. He smoked too much. His buzz cuts his mind off. He gets annoyed at how slow it's working. He almost falls down as he tries to stand up. He stubs the cigarette out in a can. It's filled with something soft. It smells like grease. The whole garage smells like lighter fluid, then smoke. He checks to see if there's a fire. He freaks out and knocks over the gas can as he turns. It dumps all over his backpack. The thing's soaked. He pulls everything out of it. He hears his mom call his name. His drawings are running. They're fucked. He spins around. He wads them up. They're lying on the floor. They flare and vanish. Everything looks blue, what with the snow and the dusk and the smoke. Everything slows down, or his mind does. He wants to cry. When he walks inside his mom says something. It was a question. He tells her he always ruins everything. He tells her that it doesn't matter. She just looks at him. She keeps cooking. He doesn't say anything. He doesn't tell her that even the simplest things are impossible for him to do right. He closes his eyes and walks upstairs. He lies down, almost throws up. He has this daydream that he can see the future. It's vague and empty. Because it's different it's a relief. Something washes over him. He doesn't know what to call it. Everything's okay. His mind sheds all the shit that has befallen it. He forgets it as he falls asleep, just some numb thing.

Peter and Beth are drinking Pepsi out of wine glasses and flicking through cable. The phone rings. It's Neeve.

Hey, did you know J?

Um, what? Yeah.

She says words. She fills Peter in on the details. He starts crying. He hands the phone to Beth. They walk outside together and don't say anything. He hugs her and squeezes his eyes shut. Everything's white. He opens them. He walks Beth to her car. They just hug. The sun's almost gone. He walks back inside. He calls Declan and tells him. Declan says that he just doesn't know what to say. After he hangs up he kicks in the guitar amp next to his bed. When his dad yells to keep quiet, Declan knocks over his drum kit and beats the shit out of it because everything means too much for him to handle.

Beth wakes up wearing her skirt and tights. She doesn't remember driving home. In the shower she feels like throwing up. She climbs into bed. She gets vertigo. The light in the room is dim. It feels dimmer. She thinks it's the sun setting. Her thoughts are bleached and scaled. Her lips taste salty. She touches her earrings. The holes are infected. She should take them out before she falls asleep. She should get a glass of water. She barely makes it to the bathroom in the middle of the night. She throws up in the toilet and on the floor. The water in the toilet's a mirror. She lies in the tub. She washes her hair. She stares at the ceiling. Lightning flashes outside. The sky cracks, she closes her eyes.

Peter drives over to J's. He sits on the couch and watches a cat walk around the room. He talks to J's mom. She says that she found J lying in bed. She says that he had just gotten home. She tells Peter he'd spent the last two nights in his room playing music and drawing. She says that she thought that that was what he was doing. Then she realized it was too quiet.

She says he was getting good at guitar, that he was promising, that she was so proud. She's shaking and sobbing. Peter hugs her and she holds him like it's the last thing there is.

Upstairs Peter finds J's notebook open facedown on his guitar. He reads lyrics for songs scrawled in J's nervous scratch. The words smear meaning across his eyes. A treasure chest sinks to the bottom of the ocean.

Beth's rewriting her script. The world's bland and empty. There's nothing here for her. She's hanging on every word that she writes. At least right now. She's thinking about J even when she's not. She watches the snow out the window. Each flake is so thick. The days are so short. The sun's setting and stuff's disappearing: the horizon, the trees, the fence. The snow will be invisible in the dark. She looks at the lights on the hills in the distance. She looks at her notebook like what she's writing means something. She's not sure what it is. She doesn't care. One thing she knows is that it's going to fail because everything does in the end.

The phone rings and Peter answers it. Declan says *hey*. He takes a breath. He tells Peter that he has this idea. He and Peter could record all of Wrapped In Plastic's songs. They could make an album to give to J's friends.

The songs would be instrumental. They'd print copies of J's lyrics. He says they kinda mean so much now.

They make plans to get together next week. Declan hopes that J's mom will give them access to all of J's notebooks. He wants to look through his drawings, for cover art.

Part 2
The Impossible Perfection

BETH:
The sun passed over the house as I sipped my coffee on the back porch. We wrestled in the bedroom and I pretended that the carpet was a sheet of lava. I pinched Peter's side and he laughed, so I kicked him in the stomach. He rolled off of me and gasped for air. The neighbors had their back light on. I rested my head on his lap as he propped himself up on his pillows. I told him that we barely survived.

I dreamed that we were driving along the coast at night: the road headed through the trees, the moon was reflected on the bay. I could barely see my notebook as I tried to write it down. After Peter left for work I unpacked a little more then went for a walk. The clouds protected the sky from the mountains. I walked past a girl my age unloading duffel bags from an old Land Cruiser. A cat hid beneath a car then scampered into a hedge. The street ran uphill, toward a forest. I passed an apartment building then an empty lot. The air was still, orange barrels were stacked at the end of the street. Grass smudged to dirt became a trail that led around them. I followed it into the forest.

I startled a doe eating berries. The air moved slowly in the moments after she took off. I jumped over puddles beneath birches and cottonwoods. The trees ended and the sky began. I came upon a grassy hill and climbed to the top. I was standing on a sidewalk. In front of me were six houses ringing a cul-de-sac. The lawns had gone to seed and I walked to the first house on the left. It was a split-level minus shingles. Little light made it inside. The floor was the night sky. I stepped on some broken glass. Crushed cans and empty cases of beer were scattered all over. The sub floor was loose and soft from the rain coming through the rotted roof. Dust'd fogged the windows.

On my way back I daydreamed that the trees rearranged themselves at night. I rode my bike to get us Thai food for dinner. We drank white wine and I tried to show Peter where the cul-de-sac was on our map. I pointed to a blob that seemed like a forest. I told him that the houses looked like they were abandoned during construction. We finished the wine on the deck. The wind blew from the bay over the mountains. I laid my fingers between his. If the sky swallowed the earth it would be so beautiful when we died.

* * *

Peter got out of bed then came back with a beer. He took a swig and handed it to me. I pressed it against my forehead and twitched my legs to get the covers untangled from around them. The fan hummed behind us and I zoned out on it.

I love you.

I love you too.

Fuck, it's hot.

We went downstairs and dragged the futon off the couch. I almost dropped it twice as we carried it to the back room. The tile was cold beneath my feet. We opened the windows. Peter blew on the top of the beer bottle then socked his shoulder against the wall as he tried to turn over. I finished the beer and looked out the window: shadows of rabbits scattered and flitted, the sky was a stencil for the moon.

The next morning I woke up kissing Peter. His lips were as soft as pillows. The sun came through the window and I wrapped my legs around Peter's waist. We chugged leftover coffee. Someone mowed their lawn. My hair stuck to my forehead as I checked my e-mail. A woodpecker sharpened its beak on our fence. Peter walked through the house and closed all the windows and blinds. He cranked the AC and ran the bath. We shivered as we took off our underwear. We climbed into the tub. Steam flocked on everything and we pretended it was winter.

* * *

The girl standing behind the easel scrunched her forehead and screwed her lips. Her model ran his fingers through his hair and tucked it behind his ears. The sun shone on her face, she took a swig from her water bottle. She pushed her glasses up on her forehead and smiled as she put her brush down. They walked out to the car parked at the curb. He leaned out the open window and kissed her. She carried the painting, then the easel, into the house. Nothing on the street moved. I went inside and dumped my ice into the sink. Later, the girl came over to the porch where I was sitting. Her name was Mira, she said.

It looks like we're neighbors.

She said she liked the way my hair was cut, the way it touched my neck. She asked if she could take my picture. She came back with a camera. The leather strap was cracked, the air smelled like cement drenched in rain. She circled me as she focused the lens. I pretended I could see the horizon. I poured her a glass of iced tea. She smiled as she sat down. I asked her where she got such an old camera. She told me that her mother is a photographer. She told me that they have cameras lying around all over the house. I told her I'd love to see a print. She said she was still learning, that she'd need her mother's help, that she'd have a print in a couple days.

* * *

Mira showed me the print: my ear, my neck, my hair, the collar of my blouse. We rode our bikes to get coffee. Her front brake made so much noise. She showed me a trail that cut across town. I had her sign the back of the print. We hugged in her driveway. I dug through a box and looked for a frame. I stood on a chair as I hung the print. I turned on the bath. I touched my toe where Peter carved our initials into the floor. In the tub I breathed heavily and pretended Peter was lying on me. I closed my eyes and slid under the surface of the water. I held my breath and shook the soap from my hair. Outside, I kneeled beside the azalea and weeded. The milk jug was filled with rain water. Peter pulled in the driveway. He watered the rosemary. I chased away a cat that'd been circling a rabbit. The wind rang in my ears. I brushed mulch off my pants as we went inside. We made out on the couch. My hair got caught in his watch band. We fell asleep with the radio on. I shook Peter until we stumbled into bed.

Mira and I played video games and drank iced tea. Link was named Mirabeth. Her print was hanging next to the couch. She asked me what I was writing when she took the picture. I told her that I was writing a story, that it was set in the cul-de-sac in the woods. I told her I was writing a paragraph about one of the houses. That it was haunted and cursed.

That night it rained in sheets. Peter turned off the lights and we looked out the windows. The wind blew the leaves off the trees. One of them fell and just missed the house. We spent the next morning sawing and stacking it. The rain continued and the leaves clogged the storm drains. Children wearing boots stomped through puddles. Water sprayed as they rode their bikes. That night I dreamed I was in the house in my story. A murderer had killed a young girl in it. Her death had cast a spell that turned the house into a black hole. I was trapped. The next morning I went for a walk after I drank my coffee. The edges of the clouds were part of the sky. My face felt damp. Someone rode a motorcycle down the street. I pictured a barn on an empty road. Later I wrote, then rewrote, a paragraph in my story. It was my dream. The narrator was a witch. She had ideas about undoing the spell that trapped her. She used a pen knife to carve a circle into the wall. She climbed through it and floated in space. Everything was a ghost of something else. The halos around the stars looked like cellophane. The light that they showed bent and scaled past her. She closed her eyes. Silence coursed around her. Everything disappeared. The end.

Mira and I went on a hike. We road our bikes to where

the trail was. It followed along the coast. A field cut through the trees. I turned my ankle on a stump. I hadn't seen it. Everything was too tall. When we stopped to eat it began to hurt. It's because I was resting it. I pulled down my sock. My ankle was all swollen and red. It felt warm. I told Mira I needed to keep moving. The path turned. It led away from the water. It was an old logging road. I stepped on crushed clam shells. Birds had dropped them. The path disappeared. It was overgrown. We headed in the same general direction. Bushes and branches snagged my skirt. They smacked Mira's legs. She stopped squinting. The trees blocked most of the light. The air got thick. I began to sweat. I brushed my bangs back. Things broke at some switchbacks. Mira ran up ahead. She was taking pictures. She looked down on me. My eyes weren't used to the light. I couldn't tell what happened. She put her camera away. There was a spot that was level. We looked out on the water. I pulled out my bottle. The warm water was okay. A cloud moved in front of the sun. An eraser wore through a piece of paper. That was the sky. I got a chill. It disappeared. Air moved against my face. Mira ran her fingers through her hair. It began to rain as we were coming down. It picked up. It made the ground damp. I giggled as I slipped and slid. Mira fell and her legs were covered with mud. When we got to our bikes we were soaked. It'd taken forever.

I could barely move my foot. I called Peter and we waited under a tree. When he picked us up we blasted the heat. Peter turned up the music. We couldn't stop laughing. A couple days later Mira showed me the pictures she'd taken. They were all green and brown. There was a picture of me. I was standing in the shade. I couldn't make me out. Mira said the sun was against me. She said it sucked. She said these were the last pictures she'd take with this camera. She said it had gotten destroyed when she fell down.

The time changed and we got up early. Peter and I rode our bikes through the fog along the water. I had a sore throat and I sipped a cup of coffee. I took a shower and hacked up phlegm. Someone read a children's story on the radio. It reduced me to tears. I chewed a bagel. Peter touched my forehead and took my temperature. He made a bed on the couch. I cried and hugged him. I told him that I loved him. I fell asleep. A day later I sat on Mira's bed as we listened to Joy Division. I sipped the tea that she'd made me. I told her it would heal me for sure. She showed me one of her photographs. She'd painted over it. The tree was blue, the hill was white. I asked her about the painting of Kevin. She said it was horrible but that he loved it, of course. She asked me how I knew I wanted to be a writer. I told her that I knew since I was little. I told her that in high school I adapted a story by my favorite writer into a script for a film. That it was the first real thing I wrote. She told me that she was thinking of writing a novel for Kevin. She wanted to know if I thought she could do it. I told her that she could do whatever it was she wanted to. I asked her what her idea was. She said it was a ghost story, but that it would also be about how much she loves Kevin. I told her that it sounded so huge and amazing. I told her the paper it was written on would blush at its greatness.

Part 3
The Enders

Mira was sitting at the table. Her feet were on the seat. Her chin was on her knees. I showed her how to chop an onion. I showed her how to sharpen a knife. She mixed yeast with water. She kneaded dough. That night Peter, she, and I ate dinner. He poured her some wine, then more. The oven heated up the entire house. All the windows were open. The fans didn't do anything. Mira said she didn't feel good. She got flushed, I gave her some water. She said that didn't help. She laid down on the couch. She said she was so dizzy. I asked her if I should call her mom. She looked at me all confused. She said her mom wasn't there. She fell asleep. I began to freak out. I snapped at Peter. I kept checking her house. It was pitch black. It looked like it wasn't there. Her parents didn't come home. I tried to work on my story. I couldn't concentrate. I didn't get anything written. I began to doze off. I checked on Mira. I looked at my notebook. I wrote a sentence then another. I closed my eyes. In my dream I was still writing. Mira's house was a model for a scene. It became part of the house in the woods. Eventually that changed. It disappeared into a black hole. It wasn't a part of anything.

When Mira woke up she said she was so embarrassed. I made her drink more water. I gave her some juice. She drank some coffee. She smiled and hugged me then walked next door. She told me she would see me later.

I sat down on the couch and spazzed out. Peter came home from work early and I cried myself to sleep. My thoughts were a forest, my brain was an avalanche. I woke up and felt calm and empty. It rained and fog rolled in. A fine spray covered the skylight as I lay in bed. I got a headache from crying. I began to sob because it was such a small thing to suffer. I rocked back and forth in the tub. My mother taught me that you're supposed to cook for people so I tried to chop an onion. It stung my fingers. I had trouble focusing my eyes. The knife chipped the enamel in the sink when I threw it. We ordered pizza and somehow I devoured three pieces. Peter drove to the store to buy me more Kleenex. He fell asleep holding me. I counted my pulse throbbing behind my eyes. I felt exhausted and sick when I woke up. Pouring a glass of water was too loud for my migraine. I threw up after taking a sip of coffee.

The chairs were arranged in rows. They'd set up a

picture of her as a baby and a pencil drawing of a tree torn from a notebook. Someone had framed the drawing. I hugged her mother. She told me they were investigating the accident. She was hoping for something. It was the way she spoke. I closed my eyes. I heard footsteps and a door opening. Cold air scrunched my shoulders. Peter put his arm around me. Kevin shook, sobbed, and stared. I didn't know what to say. The rain turned to snow as we drove home.

I turned on the TV and looked at her print hanging next to the couch. One of the speakers went out on the stereo. I drank whiskey, then vodka. It rained through the night. By morning I was dazed and hollow. Peter and I stood in the tub and washed each other's hair. I gulped water from the showerhead as I kissed him. Our hair dried while we napped. The sun set. I dreamed that I heard children playing outside.

In the spring I planted a currant because I didn't trust myself to remember forever. I dumped the clay soil next to the fence. Peter and I lay in bed. His stubble pricked the skin on my chest. We talked about money. We talked about someday having a baby.

I started to write a story about Mira. Outside the window a cat walked along a fence. Birds like dominoes. My hair grew more than I thought. I finished the story and showed it to Peter. I told him that I didn't write what happened because what happened is reality. I told him that reality is the boringest movie on the dullest screen in the world.

The Emptiest Place in the Circle

by Beth Vijar

Mira Just finished the novel she wrote for Kevin. It's an amateurish, impressionistic ghost story about a child who accidentally suffocates after locking herself in a chest in her grandmother's attic. The girl's ghost goes on to live in the attic and write a series of interrelated stories in which she examines and reimagines her own death. Mira's hope is that the spooky exterior of the story will attract Kevin enough to draw him in so that he can't help but subconsciously absorb all the love and affection she's encoded in the text. She's thinking about this, and how needy she can be, which is okay since Kevin totally loves her back when she steps off the curb and, for whatever reason, a cab's brakes fail as it enters the intersection.

Kevin's talking to Mira's ghost. She's telling him how, once you die, time is frozen and infinite and there isn't really space as such. That's how, she explains, she can be here and also be present in the afterlife. He tells her about the dream he had last night, and how she was still alive in it. Then he asks her if you dream when you're dead and she says that she dreams about being alive with him. She starts crying these weird papery tears and looks right at him. He reaches out to hug her but she disappears, like she evaporated out of that mirrory shadow she always seemed to be standing in.

Kevin's writing a sequel to the novel the police found in Mira's backpack. It's made up of a series of interrelated stories which take place in a utopian world where he and Mira's ghost can coexist. In the latest story, the whole universe disappears except for Mira's ghost and him because of a spell she cast to protect them. His parents would send him back to that therapist if they read it so, since he wants to stay off those meds, he keeps it in his locker at school. He knows it's not real though, he's not that fucked up. He just wants to create this big monument to Mira's memory or whatever. He knows in a hundred years no one will remember it. He knows the writing's shit and full of clichés, but he's going on instinct and right now this feels like the right thing to do.

CHAPTER 3
FIRST, LAST

Plato once taught that at the end of time all things will return again to where they once were.

—Jorge Luis Borges

Part 1
The Brightening Shadow

We moved to the island after our daughter died. The house we purchased was on a spit. On a map it was strung between two inlets. Our house was taller than the trees around it. We could watch cars approaching on the gravel road. Everyone on the spit kept to themselves. My wife and I were together all the time. So much went unsaid between us.

The summer was dry and in our sadness we barely unpacked. We took long walks at night. The skies were clear then, we held each other's hands. I thought that we were both breaking down inside. There grew in me a sense that it was she and I against the world. I could see my thoughts mirrored in her eyes. Sometimes she'd forget to hold it together and wake up crying. Sometimes I was stronger than was possible.

September soaked the islands and the burn ban was lifted. Smoke from the piles of burning leaves drifted through the trees and hills and into the sky. Without our jobs or Mira, our time was largely free. We slept in later and later. The house came with a pile of wood for the stove. Each day I chopped it for an hour. Every day followed the one before it. It got colder and the wind picked up. Inside my wife perfected her fire-building technique. We rarely used the furnace. At dusk she would set up her tripod and take some pictures of our backyard. The prints sat in a stack next to her side of the bed. It grew weekly. Beyond our yard was a run of blackberry bushes, then the water. A footpath led through them to it. Deer droppings appeared in the yard overnight. A thin band of light grew along the horizon each morning.

We were pelted by hail as we stood in the grass. The trees on the edge of the field loomed and shook in the wind. I could just see them falling on us. The ducks took off. We'd followed them to the pond. My jaw tightened. We ran back to the car. The sky turned from white to gray. I searched through my jacket for the keys. She stood by her door with her hands in her pockets. She pulled her hood over her hat. Her hair peeked from beneath it. When I turned the key the engine didn't turn over. The hail looked like snow on the ground. It crunched beneath our feet as we walked home. She said she wished she had her sunglasses. She brimmed her eyes with her mittened hand. The hail began to melt. It began to rain, then stopped. The temperature dropped. My face got windburned. So did the tip of her nose. At home I reached in my pockets for my keys. God knows where they were. She kept me from losing it. We climbed through an open window. She called about getting the car towed. I warmed my hands beneath the faucet. The water got too hot and I burned them. The wallpaper blurred and mirrored. I slammed the faucet and punched the wall. The sheet-rock above the coffeemaker was dented. A trace of blood was smeared on the wallpaper. I began to cry. I felt a fever come over me then pass. Somewhere in my brain was a tapestry of words and images but I wouldn't find it. I slammed our bedroom door. I buried my face in our pillows.

I walked down to the beach. There were no islands after this one. A crane traced the surface of the water. It disappeared into the distance. The ocean was an enormous mirror. It reflected space. The sun dissolved into it. It was endless and perfect. That's what the world was like when it was new. Before nature realized it couldn't sustain flawlessness. Before death ruined everything.

As long as we're together it's okay. I didn't know that

until I realized it. We knew we were pulling away from the world. If it wasn't intentional it was something we were aware of. We talked about it. She said she couldn't stand when someone in the village would try to talk to her. She said they thought they knew something about her because someone had whispered to them about Mira once. She'd barely make it back to the car to start sobbing. I felt like I should protect her but I felt incapable. I sat in the bathroom and we talked while she took a shower. I told her she should tell people to go fuck themselves.

For her birthday I built her a bird feeder painted yellow and white like our house. Thistle seeds formed a halo on the ground below it. A rat got stuck inside. I used a broom handle to get it out. It pounced on the ground then took off. The seeds disappeared from the ground over the winter. The feeder filled up with rain.

We had our life, such as it was. It wouldn't last forever, but it would last until we died, preferably together. That's what I lived in fear of not happening.

She was sitting in her chair, cleaning one of her cameras. She played with the clicky mechanisms. She pointed the camera at me. A sound like a metal rubber band. I stuck my tongue out at her. She put the camera down. I walked over to her and hugged her. I had a daydream about something impossible and perfect. It took us off the island. It brought Mira back to life. Later, we were lying in bed. She was dozing. I looked at her face. At the way it was half hidden by the lock of hair that pushed forward. At the way she didn't always look so sad when she was sleeping.

Four girls about Mira's age were standing out on the deck on the upper level of the ferry. They were wearing hoodies, sweatpants, and jeans. One of the girls had her hair pulled back into a ponytail. She was staring at the screen on her phone. She was talking.

He called, but then said he wasn't going to come out or whatever.

They sipped out of Starbucks cups and bottles of water. The wind was in their hair and the sun was in their eyes. Because they were alive I wished they were dead.

I got drunk which I never did. I was cooking dinner and there was a bottle of wine for the sauce. I walked around the house and looked out the windows. Everything was out of control. I could feel it. She was in the village so I was alone. That made it worse. I walked out to the shed to look through our boxes. I was searching for pictures of Mira and me. I knew they had to be somewhere. I had no idea where. I couldn't think straight. It seemed impossible. It was a puzzle I needed to solve. I stared forward and did nothing. I imagined that every record of Mira disappeared when she died. I started to sob. I had this idea to recreate it all. I opened a box, I was looking for something. I put the flashlight in my mouth. It helped me to see. It didn't matter though. I didn't know what I was looking for.

I had a dream about Mira. I wrote it in a letter to her: *You and I are standing in the woods looking at the sky. It's afternoon and overcast. We head forward. "There will be enough time," you say. The snow's a brittle layer over the grass. We stand staring at a river. It's a shallow trickle hemmed by snowy banks. I leap from rock to rock. I skim the surface with my boots. You're a child now, standing in a wool coat and mittens. You laugh and smile. Your lips are pink around your teeth. Your coat is blue, your scarf is red. The snow becomes invisible when it lands on your face. I tell you that I miss you so much. I want to hug you but the river is growing wider. My heart breaks because I wave goodbye to you but you don't see. The snow is falling too thickly. The sun is setting.*

A hawk stood on a fence post on the edge of a field. We walked together on a trail that ran through the field and into a forest. The trail cut a crude loop through the trees. It turned steeply toward the banks of a creek. I was worried about her ankle which she'd twisted the week before on the steps. As we came out of the trees they cast shadows that cut off at the water's edge. We both stopped walking. As a word, love fails. Winter days fleet and vanish. It was one of the days that we didn't talk about Mira, which was okay. I wasn't really thinking about her until I realized that I wasn't, so then I did. Dinner didn't taste like anything. She threw it out and we went to bed early. The sun set and the rain stopped. The puddles turned to ice. I dreamed that we were buried underground: the earth was soft and we sank through it, we never stopped. I felt hungover when I woke up. A calm came upon us. The house was a mess but that was okay. Our tiny radio only picked up French-language programming. The rooms seemed darker. I was soaking in the bath. She came in and sat on the edge of the tub. We talked about maybe watching a movie later. She said her feet were freezing. She pulled them out of her slippers and stuck them in the tub. I held her hand with my wet one. That night snowdrifts rose up to the windows and drafts passed through the house. We sat with comforters on the couch. I sipped tea and brandy. I daydreamed about a tree as I fell asleep. It was greener than reality. It grew taller than a mountain.

* * *

The bird swept down thirty feet in front of us. It took off with a black rabbit. Several more were in the grass ahead of us. When we made our way to them we saw that the rabbits were puppies. They were huddled around a large mutt with a bullet hole in her head and blood pooling out of her mouth. The puppies just lay there except for one that was pawing and trying to suckle its mother. Her blood was dried and stuck in its fur. We tried to clean it off with our jacket sleeves. My hands burned from the cold wind coming in from over the water. My fingers felt so thick. We ran back to the car with the puppy. The house of the farmer whose field we had been standing in had lights on. Smoke was coming from its chimney.

She filled a pan with warm water. He moved and squirmed in it as he warmed up. The water turned pink and brown from the blood. He tried to breathe and swallowed some of the water. He threw up milky vomit. I held him with both hands. I dried him off with a paper towel. She went online to see what we were supposed to do. We didn't have any newspapers. He fell asleep on the bed we made out of the old towels and pillows. We'd pulled them out of some boxes. None of them were Mira's. We'll never open those boxes.

Part 2
The Photographer

I felt like I was different but nothing had changed. I stood in the bathroom and stared into the mirror. I disappeared. The walls blurred and heaved. I watched as I moved through each day. I couldn't concentrate on anything for very long. I ate too much sugar. I thought that maybe it was stress. You had me take vitamins. I felt like things weren't really there. Or me. I daydreamed. I pulled back. I kept an eye on what things could become. You surprised me for my birthday. We went to the mainland. I couldn't remember what year I was born. I left my license on the island. It took us a minute. It didn't matter. We went hiking in the mountains. We huddled under a tree wearing ponchos. Our faces were slick and cold. When we got back to the cabin we used all the hot water up. You cooked dinner and we drank beer. You talked on the phone with your mother. She didn't recognize your voice. She didn't know who you were. Things lifted. We laid in bed after we ate. We made out all dizzy. You kissed me as you came. Your breath was a beery sonnet. I woke up late in the morning. It was like I hadn't slept. We rode the ferry between the islands. I forget what we talked about then. Breathing the air coming off the water just exhausted us. We sat on the deck and you held my hand. We could see for miles. It was so clear. The sky was too much to handle. You had me put on your sunglasses. You got up to pee. You came back with a bottle of water. You picked up a dollar off the deck. You walked over to the railing. You gave it to a little girl. Her mother made her say *thank you*. She hugged you. You came back to me. You were smiling. Your eyes were filled with light, if there is such a thing.

I woke up in the middle of the night. I'd had a dream that I was scared of the dark. Something was coming after me. I couldn't see it. I ran through trees then over rocks. I smashed my fingers and scraped my knees. My shoes were soaked from running through a creek. Twigs crunched and split in the distance. I kept moving. The cold air made my jaw ache. I came upon a clearing. A hut stood in the middle of it. I could see by the moon. The hut was our house. I couldn't make my way to it. The clearing grew larger and larger. The hut moved farther and farther away.

I wrote the dream down when we woke up. I talked to you. I sipped my coffee. I didn't know why my hand was shaking. I told you. That night it lashed and fractured. The wind did. Light sped through my hollow head. I had the same dream again. I woke up exhausted. You washed the soap out of your mug in the sink. I told you that it didn't mean anything. You said my brain was haunted like a house. All afternoon I thought about the dream. I felt so sad. I decided to photograph some trees. I thought that maybe it would calm me. I rode my bike south from the spit. The road led up into the hills. They rolled away from the water. My legs burned. Steam rose from the grass. It was the sun. Trees ran along a ridge above me. I left my bike leaning against a boulder. I sipped water and coughed. Blood ran to my head. The air was damp and cold in the trees. The sun was a shadow behind them. Things felt clean. I sat down next to some salal. I sucked the skin off a berry. The damp of the soil soaked through my skirt. I brushed pine needles off my butt. I dried my hands on the front of my skirt. I removed my cameras from their cases. I took a picture of a creek running over rocks and roots. The water was invisible when I printed it. I half knew it would be. The sun came through the trees. Light showed on a fern. I ate my sandwich and sipped my tea. I had warmed. I rode back without a hat or jacket. I sketched in my notebook at the table. It was a river. The current was separate from the water. My wrist smeared the ink as it dried. My grass-stained fingertips left prints where I touched the paper.

I pictured Mira's accident. It happened over and over. It made me regret every minute that I had been alive. I based so much off the car. It was an answer to a question I should never have had to ask. When we saw it we were the only people in the lot. The attendant just left us there. They'd towed it on a trailer. It was the only thing there. Later one of the police came. You went through the car with him. It was a mess. You took some CDs, a pack of gum. I finally walked up to the car. I thought that it smelled like her. That was the last thing I needed. I had to walk away. I had to tear through something. I kicked at the gravel. Mud stuck to the toe of my shoe. Blood and hair decorated the windshield.

I tried to talk to you about it. I said that I had to. You told me to just shut up. You stormed off and slammed the door. I ran after you. I rested my forehead against the door. You didn't say anything. I begged you to come out. When I opened the door you were asleep. Your face was bloated and red. I walked through the house and locked the doors. I shut off the lights and it was as dark as it was outside.

I raked around the woodpile before it rained. I rooted something out. The dog chased it. He cornered it against the fence. I heard a squeal and hissing. I smacked him on the head with the rake. I kneeled down. A mole was on its back. It was twitching in the shallow. It was covered with mud. I dragged the dog inside. I growled as I threw him. I was winded back in the yard. The mole had stopped moving. It looked smaller. You found me a shoebox in the shed. I put the mole in it. You dug a hole. You cut through the dock roots with the shovel. You said it was almost too much. I ringed the hole with rocks and stones. You said that I should have just tossed it. I told you that I had to do it. I told you that I had to.

October was overcast. The rain made it feel colder than it was. My foot fell asleep when I sat. I walked stiffly. Things moved forward: water rose in the ditch beside the road, mildew specked the windowsill. We walked the dog in the dark. Puddles mirrored the night sky. I felt calm. Things held together. My eyes began to change. It was impossible to see anything close up. Light began to hurt them. I had to squint in order to read. I walked around the house in my socks. It got so quiet at night. I watched out the window. My thoughts clung together. I made out shapes in the dark. I don't know if they were there. I would drink beer and fall asleep on the couch. I'd wake up crying after you turned off the lights.

* * *

You got up early and changed the oil. It got all over your face. Your hair was a mess. You had to take a shower. You asked me to look for something in your eye. I got hyper. I told you that I needed a bike ride. I rode to the middle of the island. Something like seven miles. The sign said *private road*. The road became a path. It crested in a circle of brown earth and trees. Set back in the clearing was an old A-frame. It looked closed up. Behind it was a meadow. Everything in the house hung in shadows. I took a picture of the front of it. I had a daydream that it was the hut from my other dream. I climbed a tree that was hollow and dead from woodpeckers. I took a shot of the sun hitting the window. I ended up reflected in the second-story window. I climbed down the tree and rang the doorbell. I tried the door. Everything was still and covered with dust. I walked to the window and moved the curtain. I took a picture of the clearing. Something sprung from behind the couch. A cat pounced on something that wiggled, a rat. Blood-smeared on the tile beneath the table. I heard a sound coming from the loft. I said *hello*. I walked up the stairs and saw a rat tail disappear behind a wall. When I turned the corner I threw up in my hand. Ten or so rats squirmed and gnawed between the exposed ribs of a German shepherd, its face and tail intact and stiff, its eyes frozen open.

* * *

You called the police for me. Animal control removed the cat. They were volunteers. They used fishing net. No one knew who the house belonged to. Records were looked into. I called to check on the cat. The woman said it would live. She said that it was dehydrated, that it had worms. They'd put it on an IV. The owner of the house had just disappeared. There would be an investigation. There were no known relatives. You held me that night as we lay in bed. I told you all I could think about was the German shepherd. Animal control had said it probably starved to death. I sobbed uncontrollably. The dog hated when I cried. He just sat and looked at me. I tried to hug him. I drank a beer in bed as we fell asleep. We forgot to turn off the lights. When I woke up at 3 they were still on. I nudged you to turn yours off but you didn't respond.

They flew you to a hospital on the mainland in a helicopter. I spent every day with you. I sat beside you. I had a nurse take our picture on your birthday. You can see my face reflected in the window. The hospital put it in their newsletter. A short paragraph was published with the photograph. The writer hadn't been here. He hadn't seen you. I threw the paper away. I had in my mind that it was cursing you, that you were held in stasis because of its presence. I talked to you.

I read you this as I wrote it. I became mindful of each moment. I drew lines in my notebook to keep track of the days, but I didn't need to because they were all the same.

They moved you to a rehab facility back on the island. Nothing else could be done, the doctors said. We flew toward the sun before we landed. There were no names for the colors. I rested my hand on your knee. I held your hand. I pretended that you held mine back. Wind blew the tree limbs in a storm. I cried then stopped. It was ridiculous. Something shattered. There was a bookshelf in your room in the center. It was filled with magazines, games, and decks of cards. The walls were carpeted up to my waist. I watched out the window. The sky was white above the trees. Things looked warmer as the afternoon bore onwards. The light split into bands and stripes. Dust hung in the air. I argued about the dog. The facility relented. He ambled up on the bed and cradled behind your knee. I looked at your face for something. Nothing. Over time your lips grew dried and cracked. The center was on the edge of the village. The only noise at night was the sound of the cars driving off of the ferry, but you couldn't hear them.

I took your picture every day. I stood with my knees against the footboard. I used the camera that you bought Mira. A blurry shadow hung in front of the lens. I stopped looking at the photos and just saved them to the computer. Then one day I lost the cable. Someday the hard drive will crash and the camera will die and they'll be gone. It doesn't matter though, because I'll remember you even when I'm dead.

I began to notice the time change in the summer. My armpits sweated. The sun set later and later. The night was a mirror. I grabbed the lampshade and tilted it toward me. I looked at your face. I imagined looking into your eyes. They could see me. It was like something was there. I shook my head. A thought trembled on my lips. It was some old memory: you were drinking too much. I thought that meant you didn't love me. I don't know. I was going to take off with Mira. For whatever reason, we got into a fight and I broke your nose. Blood poured down your face. You fell asleep in the car as I drove you to the hospital. You started to cough up blood. I was so worried. When you opened your eyes I saw them shining in the light. In the hospital we stood at the desk. I stared into my purse. I looked for something. Mira was hanging from your neck like a cape. You put your arm around me. You had a black eye. Mira put a bandage over your nose. She fell asleep lying across our laps when we sat down. I just wanted to make it till tomorrow. I just wanted to be with you.

* * *

A nurse walked into the room. She was holding a clipboard. She was checking something. I read the magazine next to me. She wrote something down. I looked out the window. Someone parked their car. A cat lay in the ivy. It licked its paw. It stopped moving. The nurse turned around and smiled. She set the clipboard down. She put the pen in her pocket. I looked away. She started to talk, walk toward me. She called me by my name. I nodded. I listened to what she said. The words were just words. They were supposed to mean something. I didn't believe it. I ignored whatever I heard. It didn't change anything.

I would forget to eat or drink. I got headaches. The nurses reminded me. They brought me a small pitcher of water. The pain relievers I took upset my stomach. I became nauseous and found that I was unable to eat. I sipped chamomile tea. It barely helped. I got weak and tired at night. I ate bread and margarine and drank lager. The dog licked the crumbs and oil from my plate. His tail knocked my beer glass over. I put food in his bowl. My head spun as I lay in bed. I vomited blood. I barely slept and never dreamed. My thoughts ranged.

I don't know what I'll do without you. I don't want, or know, how to say it. So I won't think about it. The world's a tunnel, I only see you. My thoughts are filtered and blinded. Concern will lift from my shoulders. We will be subsumed by the world. I'll wait for your eyes to open, which is impossible, but so is the opposite.

I held a picture of you at arm's length and squinted. Your muscles slackened and your face changed. Your temples became grayer, your hair thinner. I wasn't scared to shave you anymore. The nurse had showed me. When I nicked you nothing happened. Just blood. It dried and scabbed. It flaked away. I combed your hair back after it was washed. I dried out your ears with Q-tips and alcohol. I was worried about infections. I sat sideways on the chair. The arm supported the back of my knees. When I closed my eyes time passed in moments instead of hours. You had a series of strokes on a Saturday and Sunday. Something in the world dissolved. Everything was changed. Monday morning was worse. It was horrible when they removed the feeding tube. Everything was what it was. That meant you were dead. Or basically. If I'd taken a picture of you I'd never have looked at it. I'm sorry I didn't put a bullet in your head like I always promised I would.

Sometimes I pretended you were alive. Those days were

lost. I stood in the front hallway and cried. A pod of orcas vanished without explanation that summer. The news said they were migrating; their carcasses started washing up half-decayed. Nothing could be explained. A doctor came to see me. He gave me pills. I flushed them down the toilet. I got obsessed with a tree falling and crushing the house. I worried about what would happen to the dog if I died. I climbed a ladder and stood on the roof. I studied the trees. In bed I kept worrying but I tried to ignore it. I had the dream about the clearing again. It was different. I wrote it down. A witch walked into it. It was empty. She picked up a mask from the ground. It was made from wicker and covered with leaves. When she put it on, time rushed and swam. It was winter in the clearing and the whole world was different. You and Mira were alive. We didn't live on the island. I didn't have to be alone. Everything was okay and it always would be.

Part 3
An Ocean Shaped Like Your Mind

I. The Photographer's Husband

A year later: she drove through the woods. The tires kicked up oil and gravel from the road. Cold wind swept over the bay and ran through the trees. The headlights disappeared into the rain. Beyond the water the sun was rising. The moon was a cloud. A bird flew straight at the windshield. Maybe it was a bat. She didn't swerve or slow down. A creek stirred along the side of the road. A plastic bottle bobbed in the foam. I watched her as she drove. She stared forward. I could see the bones in her hands. They were lit by the dashboard. There was something that I needed to say but I couldn't say it. I invented a way. It didn't work. I should have known. The car slowed down. I got dizzy. I opened my eyes. We crossed a bridge. I looked at her. I wanted to take care of her. I tried to touch her hand. I gave up hope. I tried not to cry. I told myself it didn't matter, that the world was all broken anyway. I told myself it was destroyed. She pulled the car into the driveway and stopped. She stood in the yard in her socks. Her arms were wrapped around her waist. I looked at her face. Her eyes were a haunted house. The world was a ghost. I followed her into the kitchen. It smelled like vinegar. She gulped a glass of water. Her feet were sopping wet. I stood in front of her. There was nothing there. She rested her hand on the cupboard. The faucet needed to be fixed. It was dripping. She walked outside. I looked at the clock, then out the window. The white sky sprayed pale mist and I watched Margaret as she stood and wept.

II. Margaret, a Year Later/Culter

I had dreams that you died differently. I had them every night. They were all different, but they were all the same. In my drowsy waking I imagined you holding me. Then you disappeared. I woke up crying. I tried not to sleep. I thought that then I wouldn't dream. I looked out the window as I sat in the chair. I drank coffee. The sky was clear. The planets were the bright lights, the stars were whatever bland distraction. The nights were cold. I didn't turn on the furnace. I thought that then I would stay awake. I could last one day. Any more and I fell apart. I heard voices as I closed my eyes. They were nothing. I knew when I heard them that I would fall asleep. They were in my dreams then. When I woke up I wrote them down. At first they didn't mean anything. Over time they became something. They came together. I changed every word. A narrative formed. I created a cause. I identified an enemy. I spent time working on the writing. I had no end in sight. Over time I forgot about the dreams. I had them less and less, or maybe I stopped remembering them. It didn't matter. I didn't feel any differently. I finished the story. It was a gift to you. I don't know why. It was just writing. I did it compulsively until it wasn't compelling. I told you this in my head. I told you that you would hate it, that you wouldn't understand it. I told you not to worry, that it didn't mean anything, that nothing did.

Sarin

by Margaret Kroftis

They sat in the leader's apartment on chairs and the floor. One of them rang a chime. The leader closed his eyes. Explosions bloomed inside them. They drowned his mind in light. The adherents all watched him. He placed his glass on the carpet next to his chair. Cold air blew through the open window. A bus drove through a puddle outside. He held his breath. Complex shadows came together on the wall. They dissolved. His palms rested on his thighs. The vein on the back of his hand pulsed in time with his breathing.

He spoke: He told them that time had a beginning and an end. He told them that time and existence were the same thing. He told them that when existence ends so will all suffering and violence. He told them that they could deliver themselves and everyone else from those oppressions. He told them that it would be so.

The cult bought an old farm in the foothills of the mountains. They built sheds and huts in a fallow field. Fog hung in the old-growth pines. They built a footbridge over the river that crossed their property. It washed away when the water rose at the end of the summer. Fishing became impossible because of the eroded banks. They canned vegetables to save for the winter. They stored apples and potatoes in bins underneath their floorboards. They taped sheets of wax paper over all of their windows. Candles were allowed to burn for only one hour each night. A nutria died in their well and they couldn't drink the water for several months.

The adherents had primarily come from affluent backgrounds and the cult acquired large amounts of wealth. Money was spent publishing the leader's writings. The vagueness of his message was compelling to some. It eradicated that which overwhelmed them. The cult continued to grow. The families of some of the adherents threatened legal action. The cult's tax status was changed. The farm was sold and the cheap and secluded real estate on the island was purchased. The adherents learned how to homestead. The remaining ties with their previous lives were cut.

The leader had a dream: something triggered something that triggered something. He leapfrogged forward and drank in the aftermath. He woke in one of the small sheds that ringed the perimeter of the clearing. He walked outside and collected a bucket of snow. He melted it over a camp stove. He washed his face in the water. He drew a breath. It braced against the air. He got dressed and walked through the compound. He ate rice and drank soup with everyone else. After the meal he assigned duties and gave instructions. He left for the mainland. A week later he arrived with an old moving truck. The door on the trailer was locked. A shipping container arrived a couple days later. The leader drove the truck into the container and locked it. No one asked the leader any questions. The container remained locked for some time.

They opened the door to the pole building. A line of light cut the cement slab in two. They herded the sheep and dogs inside. They set up a video camera in the corner to record everything. The sheep huddled in a group. The dogs were scared and splintered. They nipped and circled. One of the adherents knocked the canister over with a broom handle and slammed the door. The liquid spilled and evaporated. The animals choked and convulsed. The puppeteer slackened his strings: the animals fell limp where they stood. It took the rest of the day to haul their bodies to the end of the field. It took the rest of the week for their bodies to burn through completely.

The two adherents had the same dream: light shredded the world. It skinned and organized it. They woke up in the dark and met at the gate. They followed the path down the hill. The grass had been flattened by the snow. Their noses ran in the cold. When they came upon the creek they followed it. When it forked in the woods they went right. Spring felt like autumn, they thought. They reached the village. The river hit the bay. The adherents walked into the library. They removed the canisters from their backpacks, they spilled the liquid across the tile floor. The adherents and the librarians fell. There was one other person in the room. He was standing at the computer kiosk looking something up. He fell more slowly. He went into a coma. Something in his brain protected him. No one will ever know. It was grace of a type. They flew him to the mainland. They said it was the only chance he had. Nothing happened. She sat and watched him die as he lay in the hospital. He disappeared slowly. She did everything that she could. It was nothing. She slept by his side. She dreamed that she was able to cry. There was this storm. The wind uprooted the trees, they pulled down the wires. The power was off for something like thirty seconds. When it came back on she screamed at the nurses. They told her to calm down. That was the beginning of the end. The way she saw it, his brain had been starved. She sat there and watched his slow decline. He developed pneumonia. The doctor said it would run its course. She couldn't bring herself to do

> anything. Without antibiotics the infection spread. She wrote a novel in her head. It was the same sentence on every page: *I already miss you*. When his heart stopped she was shaken. She attacked the doctor as she screamed. The nurses had to pull her off.

The floorboards creaked as the house settled in the wind. I touched where my hand had been. I drew in the heat. I was swept up in its wake. Each moment hovered and sank. Each moment slipped by. I counted every step that I took. I was walking toward the table. I was falling down. I built a bridge in my mind. I pulled myself up. The dog slumped beneath my feet. I listened to the radio. I closed my eyes. My fingers kept time on the arm of the chair. There was a tambourine in the reverb. My leg twitched. I ran across the room. I kneeled in front of the toilet. I heaved forward and sobbed. I pulled a towel off the counter and wrapped it around my shoulders. My eyes were closed. I slept on the tile. I woke up. I drew in my notebook. The pictures were mostly landscapes. They all looked the same: the horizon was just a line. I looked in the mirror. I was peaked and ripped. My eyes were black holes. I tacked my drawings to the wall. I took some pictures of them. Nothing stuck. I tore them down. I took an aspirin from the bottle. I rolled it around in my mouth as it dissolved. Something white coated my lips. My teeth chattered. I cooked mushrooms and ate them with toast and beer. I fell asleep at the table. Once it got dark the house got so cold. I woke up close to dawn. I couldn't handle it. I took my temperature. I lay in the bath to warm up. I splashed cold water on my face. I turned up the furnace and walked upstairs.

I lay in bed for a week. I barely let the dog out. I slept but didn't dream. I was weak for a month after that. I thought that I had the flu. I didn't know what it was. It took it out of me. I stood on the back porch on my toes and watched the waves as they rolled and crested then disappeared. I wiped my eyes with my sleeve. I smelled the gin as it evaporated from my glass. I followed the dog from room to room. I heated food on the stove. Broth or something. I ate a little. I sat down and closed my eyes. My chin fell forward. The light and the air combined. I got déjà vu. The thought held. The furnace hummed in the garage. I yawned. I walked upstairs. My hand came away from the banister. I tapped my thigh. The dog came up. I stood in the center of the stairs. I slumped in the corner. The sun moved faster than the moon. The air was cold and wet. Drafts came in through the windows. My eyes burned and my nose ran. The bookcase downstairs fell forward. It crashed to the floor. That was me. There was a message there but I didn't know who to. The next day I kicked the books against the wall. Over time dog hair piled up around them. Dust hung in the air when I turned on the lights. The dog walked into the room. He stood by the books and panted. He sniffed at the cracked bindings. There wasn't anything there.

III. Writer

I wrote a novel for you and Mira. It came to me quickly. I had this idea that it would be a monument to your memory. One day it just felt like the only thing I could do. I wrote it over a couple months. I pushed the old table into the spare room upstairs. It ended up in the corner. I had to the draw the blinds in order to focus. There was something about the light. I wrote by hand in a notebook. The dog lay at my feet. He panted in the heat. I opened the door for him. There wasn't anything else I could do. He wouldn't go downstairs. The book meant so much to me. You always said how I got obsessed. It became longer than I had planned on. All I did was write. The sameness of each day was compelling. I heard the dog drinking out of the toilet. I realized that I hadn't fed him in god knows how long. I had a headache. My nose was running. I drank a glass of juice as I poured his kibble into a bowl. I lay on the floor and hugged him after he ate. The rug was concentric circles. He began to squirm. I finished the book soon after that. I had worked on each sentence until it was as clear as possible, until the meaning hung in front of me. The last thing I wrote was the dedication. It said, *I miss you, David and Mira.* It reduced me to tears. After I was done the book was still all that I could think about. I zoned out as I looked out the window. It wasn't fall yet. I pictured everything covered in snow. I imagined the world was covered by ice. I blinked, shook my head. I pretended the novel was a spell, that there was something hidden within it. It would bring you and Mira back to life. I started to cry. I knew it would fail. The publisher wanted to use one of my photographs as the cover art. It was of the two of you. You were standing in front of our old house. You were looking at each other. Neither of you were looking at the camera. The hood of your parka hid your face. You could see your eyes reflected in the rear window of our car. The rest of your face was blurry. Rain had done something to the lens. Nothing turned out right. There was a bird flying over the house. It was just a smear. My voice cracked when I talked to the publisher. I said that there was no connection between my writing and my photography. I asked them if they were publishing my novel because of my photographs. A headache stretched behind my eyes. I felt like I needed to protect you and Mira. I needed to keep you hidden. It was so important. It must've come through in my voice. The book had a plain cover when it was published. It was just letters on a background. It was fine.

I called the novel *Thousand.* In it a photographer's husband and daughter die in a violent accident. She moves to an island and lives cut off from the rest of the world. After years of mourning she begins to write a novel. In her novel a young girl dies. After years of grief the girl's mother has a stroke. She goes into a coma. Her husband is left alone. He spends all his time at her bedside. He spends all his money attempting to heal her. Every possible therapy is tried. Insurance doesn't cover much. When it becomes apparent that she will never improve he begins to a write a play. In the play a princess dies. Her father falls into a deep sadness. He demands that his kingdom mourn her death. He has salt poured on all the fields. He has all the animals slaughtered. Per his edict no work can be done. The vegetables drop and shrivel. Weeds overcome the fields. There are no staple crops to eat. The animal carcasses rot. Rodents begin to thrive. Their numbers increase. Starvation and illness take hold of the kingdom. The king becomes ill. He begins to die. To alleviate his suffering on his death bed, his physician begins to tell him a story. In the story a king's daughter dies. In his grief he devises an elaborate plan to memorialize her death. He has his city destroyed and all of its inhabitants, including himself, killed. He has a new city built over the remains. For hundreds of years the city is left empty. It's forgotten. It becomes overgrown by the surrounding forest. Eventually it's discovered. Smaller then larger groups settle it. Over time settlers clear away all the vegetation. They move into its empty buildings. In the middle of the city they find a theater. In the theater they find a script for a play and instructions on its production. The king had written the play. Language has changed, but they comprehend it. The last scene leads into the first. In the play time begins and moves quickly. The world comes into existence. Millions of years pass in several seconds. A writer is writing a novel about her daughter. She had died after being in a car accident. She had been in a coma for several months. Before she died she had been writing a novel. The novel was a series of ghost stories. Combined they formed a spell. Its intention was never revealed. She hadn't gotten that far. Her mother is paying her tribute in her book. In it her daughter dies in a labyrinth. The girl's ghost is trapped in it. Over time it's forgotten. A forest overgrows it. The trees block all the light. The girl's ghost is lonely. She's filled with grief. She wanders through the labyrinth. She begins to pretend that it's growing. She imagines new paths. She sketches them in the dirt with her finger. They quickly wear away in the wind.

In her mind the new labyrinth will cut through the forest. She pretends it will cover the whole world. She continues to draw paths in the dirt. One of the series of lines she draws is a spell. It's inadvertent. It triggers something. The labyrinth becomes darker and colder. The sun explodes. The earth is destroyed. Space lingers empty. Time ceases to exist. Something random happens. Matter comes together. Another planet is formed.

IV. 3 Dreams

1

A cloud did something to the sky. It peeled back. You and I were everywhere.

2

We were up on the mountain. Mira was little. It was snowing. The light was coming from all over. We shielded our eyes but it was too bright. We got lost. You were holding Mira's hand. She was dragging her sled behind her. She had cried till we let her bring it. We knew she'd be too scared to use it. We came upon some trees that shouldn't have been there. We were turned around. The wind blew ice against our faces. Mira was wearing your sunglasses. Her hat was holding them in place. I tried to figure it out. I tried to get us back to the parking lot. You smiled as I messed with my compass. Mira was wearing lipstick. She had wanted to get dressed up. Her hair had been perfect. We spent half an hour finding someplace for her to pee. She was scared to take her tights off. You and I argued about how much I had let her drink. I found someplace for her in a run of firs. Somebody on cross country ski's helped us find our way back to the trail. You offered him a ride into town. Mira tried to walk like she was skiing. She kept asking him if she could touch the ice that had formed on his beard. When we got to town we bought a Christmas tree. Mira jumped up and down as you set up the stand. She said it was her favorite time all year. She dragged the boxes of decorations into the living room. She fell asleep on the couch as we figured out how to get the tree inside. We decorated it for her. She had made her bed on the couch. We didn't wake her up.

3

I was casting a spell. It would bring you back to life. I needed to complete a series of small actions. They were all part of it. I touched the quarter on my bed table. I spun it like a top. I dropped it on the floor. I focused on the sound. I scribbled on a piece of paper for as long as it rang. I stared at the drawing. It went blurry, then clear. I turned the paper over. I began to write a story. In the story I was driving through the woods. It was night. The road ran straight. The trees flickered past the windows. The asphalt wore and crumbled. It became gravel and dirt. A fallen tree blocked the road. I continued on foot. The trees closed in around me. The road became a path. It came out of the trees. The rain was everywhere. The sun had risen. The trees were painted flames. The sky was something that overcame them. I continued to walk. My boots flattened fallen leaves. I took a breath. The wind picked up. I could hear it in the trees. It was impossible to see what with the rain. I followed the path into the forest. It lead through them to some building. When I came closer I could see it was our house. It was worn and ripped. The paint thinned over the siding. The wood was splintered. The trees blocked the sun out. The house was completely in the dark. I blew on my palms and rubbed them together. I looked in the front window. It was caked with dried spiderwebs. I scratched at the surface. It was covered with rust and mold. I leaned on it and the frame crumbled. The window fell inward and shattered. I climbed through it. All the rooms were empty. The furniture was covered with dust and dirt. The carpet was damp and soiled. The air was thick. I started to sneeze and cough. The kitchen was damp. Dark water stood in puddles. Mildew specked all the windows and sills. The cabinets were crumbling, mushrooms were growing inside. The light coming through the windows made the room look blue even though everything outside was gray. I was shaking. I walked upstairs. You were lying on the floor in the middle of the hall. Your hair fell back from your face. I started to cry as I warmed your hands in mine. I parted your lips with my finger. I kissed you. Something happened in my head, a throb, an explosion. Everything moved forward. Everything became elevated. The house turned darker. Branches ran against the windows. Shadows fell on the walls and your face. I lay down next to you. I held you as I closed my eyes.

V. Ghoster

I pretended that you were a ghost. You were with me. You watched everything I did. I began to write so that I could tell you things. Nothing happened. I was filled with anxiety. I couldn't think straight. Nothing was interesting to me. I stopped taking photographs. I gave all of my equipment to the high school. I kept Mira's cameras though; I put them in the boxes in the closet with her paintings and clothes. I stood in the closet and pressed my forehead against the boxes. The walls weren't insulated. I could feel the cold pass through my clothes. I closed my eyes. It was darker than it was. I pretended it was empty. I pretended there was no reason to be there. I destroyed it all one afternoon.

I was overcome. I tore through the box lids with a Stanley knife. The boxes flipped and bounced when I threw them. They spilled open. The paintings ended up shredded. I threw the cameras down the stairs one by one. I fell down and screamed. My knee smashed my hand. I held onto something. I let go. My screaming bothered the dog. He paced back and forth. Something got caught in his paw. He tracked blood all over the house. I chased him as he limped. Eventually he let me look at it. He ducked and growled. I grabbed his collar when he snapped at me. I pulled a piece of metal out. I smeared the cut with Vaseline. I yelled at him when he licked it. I wrapped his paw in strips of cloth. I cut them from some old T-shirt. He bounded when he walked. His claws made this sound on the tile. He bunched and crushed an old pillow against the wall. His ears pricked and he stared. He chewed at the bandage. I woke up in the middle of the night. He was vomiting string. I tried to push his ears back. He shook and heaved. He glanced at the space where my hand had been. I got him water and scrubbed at the carpet. My hair fell forward; I tucked it back behind my ear. The room smelled like lavender soap. My finger stung when the water splashed on it. The tip of it was black and blue. The nail was hanging off. I began to sob. I tried to tell myself to stop but I couldn't. I didn't know what to say. I didn't know how to say it.